Gramercy Park

Timothée de Fombelle and **Christian Cailleaux**

EURO COMICS
ENGLISH EDITION · GRAPHIC NOVELS

An imprint of IDW PUBLISHING

EuroComics.us

EDITOR Dean Mullaney • ART DIRECTOR Lorraine Turner
TRANSLATION Edward Gauvin

EuroComics is an imprint of IDW Publishing
a Division of Idea and Design Works, LLC
2765 Truxtun Road • San Diego, CA 92106
www.idwpublishing.com • EuroComics.us

IDW Publishing
Chris Ryall, President, Publisher, & COO
John Barber, Editor-In-Chief • Cara Morrison, Chief Financial Officer
Matt Ruzicka, Chief Accounting Officer • Jerry Bennington, VP of New
Product Development • Lorelei Bunjes, VP of Digital Services
Justin Eisinger, Editorial Director, Graphic Novels & Collections
Eric Moss, Senior Director, Licensing and Business Development

Ted Adams and Robbie Robbins, Founders

ISBN: 978-1-68405-550-0
First Printing, October 2019

Distributed to the book trade by Penguin Random House
Distributed to the comic book trade by Diamond Book Distributors

Originally published in France by Gallimard Jeunesse.
Gramercy Park Copyright 2018 Gallimard Jeunesse.
Translation © the Library of American Comics LLC and Idea and Design Works, LLC.

Special thanks to Sylvain Coissard, Justin Eisinger, and Alonzo Simon.

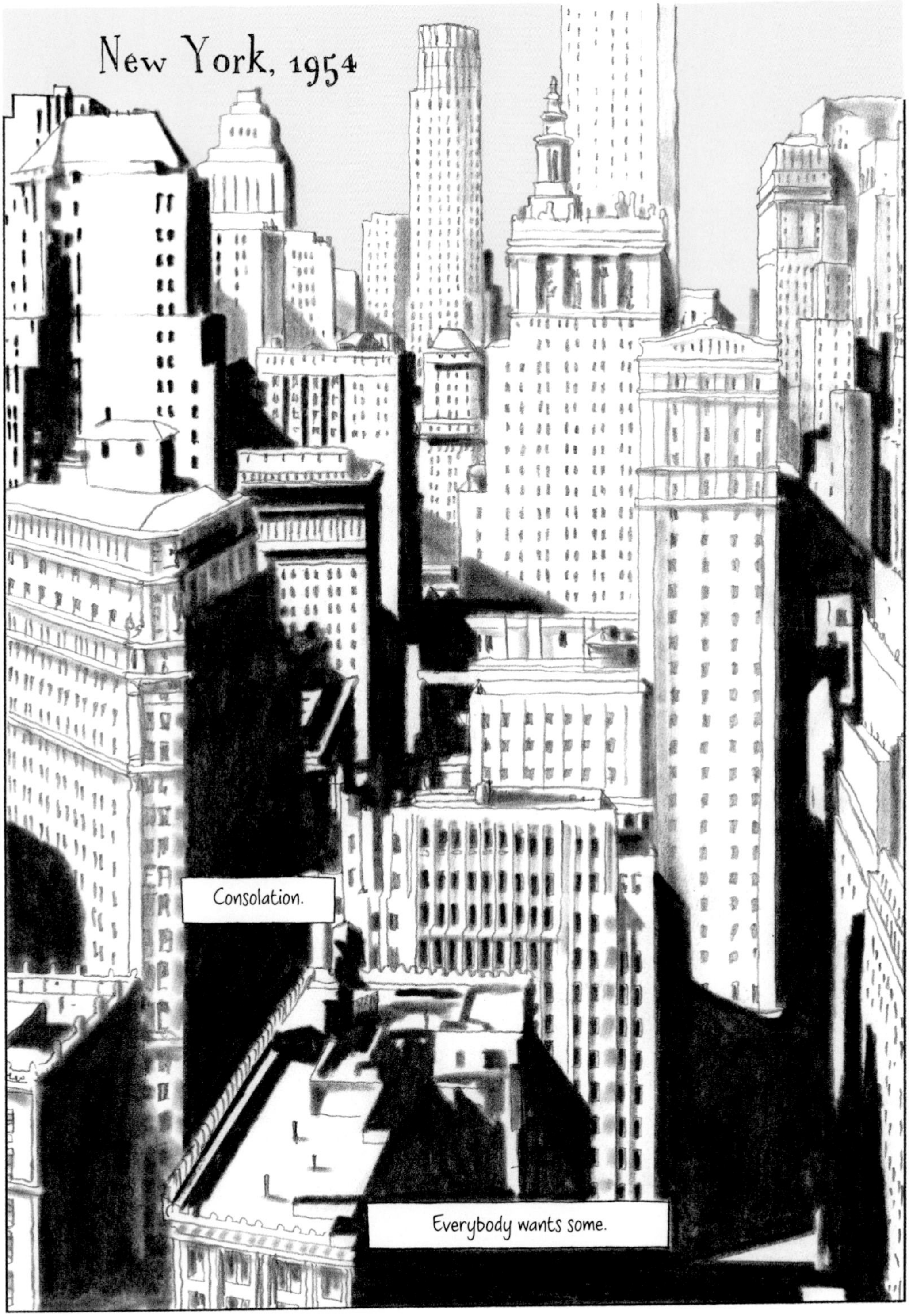
New York, 1954
Consolation.
Everybody wants some.

I know a bit about them, now. I've been watching them for a while.

People.

They want to feel better.

Consolation...

...I went looking for some among the bees.

I've been told people used to fill open wounds with honey to promote healing.

I thought the bees would save me from grief.

Saved by their patience...

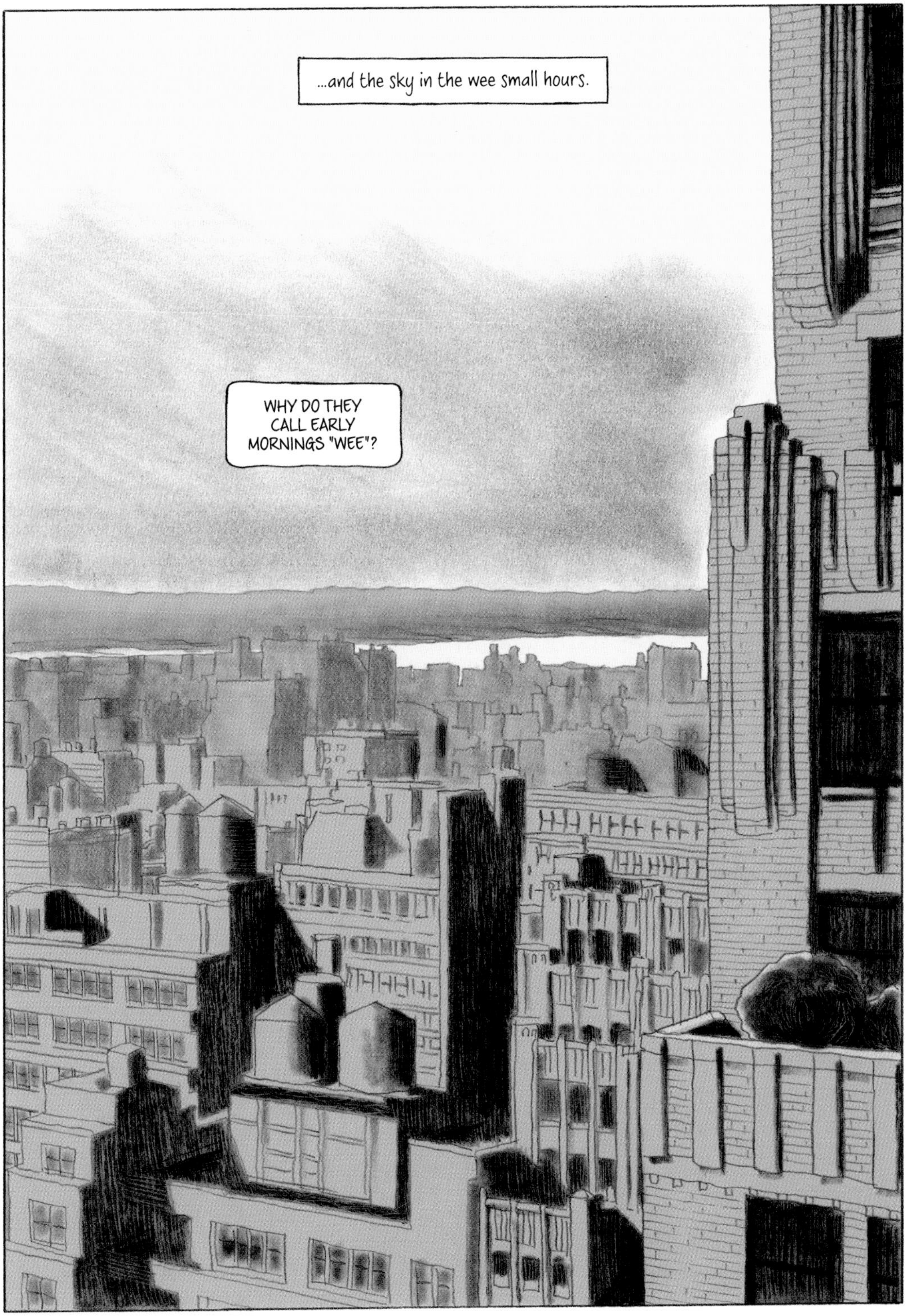
...and the sky in the wee small hours.
WHY DO THEY CALL EARLY MORNINGS "WEE"?

They draw his curtains back at nine on the dot.

He stays in his bedroom until midday.

Men come by to talk to him in the morning...

...and women at night.

Sometimes I stay hidden until night falls. The windows are open in the summertime.

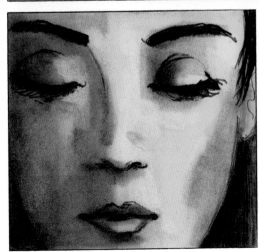

I take the last train home.

My grandfather had hives in Paris, before the War.

AND THEN?

THEN TWO FAIRIES CAME TO SEE THE WEEPING PRINCE.

AND?

THE PRINCE WASN'T DANCING ANYMORE. HE HELD HIS SLIPPERS IN ONE HAND. THE FAIRIES WHIRLED AROUND HIM.

WHY?

I DON'T KNOW.

IF HE'S SAD, THEY SHOULD LEAVE HIM ALONE!

AND NOW?

THEY'VE TURNED OUT THE LIGHTS. IT'S OVER.

THEN COME HELP ME.

11

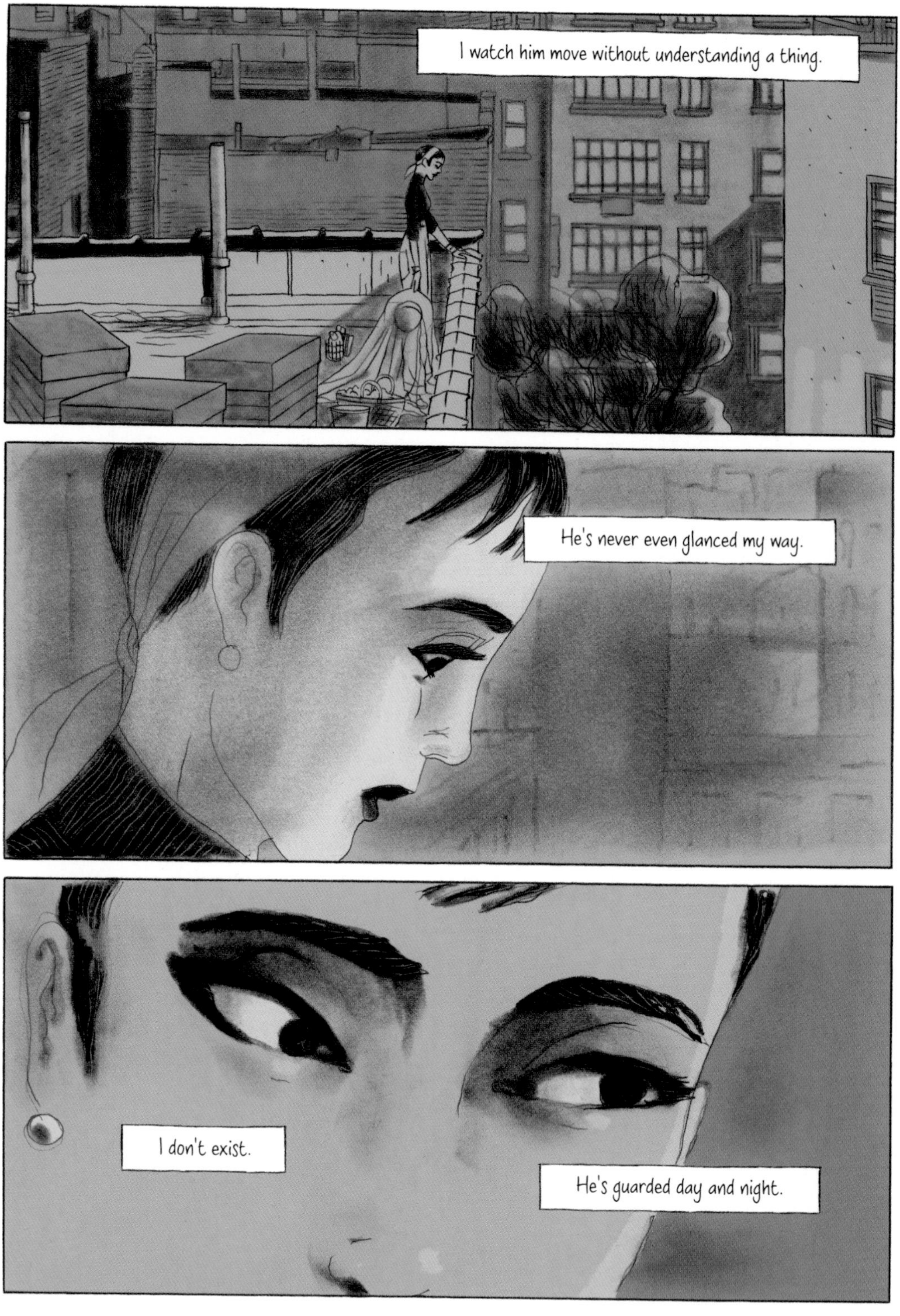
I watch him move without understanding a thing.
He's never even glanced my way.
I don't exist.
He's guarded day and night.

TUCK YOUR FEET UNDER THE CHAIR.

IT'S CRAMPED

AND THESE CRUMBS?

BLAME BLUMENFELD. HE'S ON NIGHT SHIFT. HE EATS DONUTS.

ANYTHING HIDDEN IN YOUR POCKET?

NOPE.

ALL RIGHT THEN.

THEY'VE GOT WAREHOUSES UNDER THE BRIDGE, SIR. BARBED WIRE.

AND DOGS.

A SHIPMENT'S COMING IN MONDAY. I KNOW BECAUSE MY SISTER'S SLEEPING WITH THEIR DRIVER.

WHO?

MY SISTER.

BRETT.

YES, SIR.

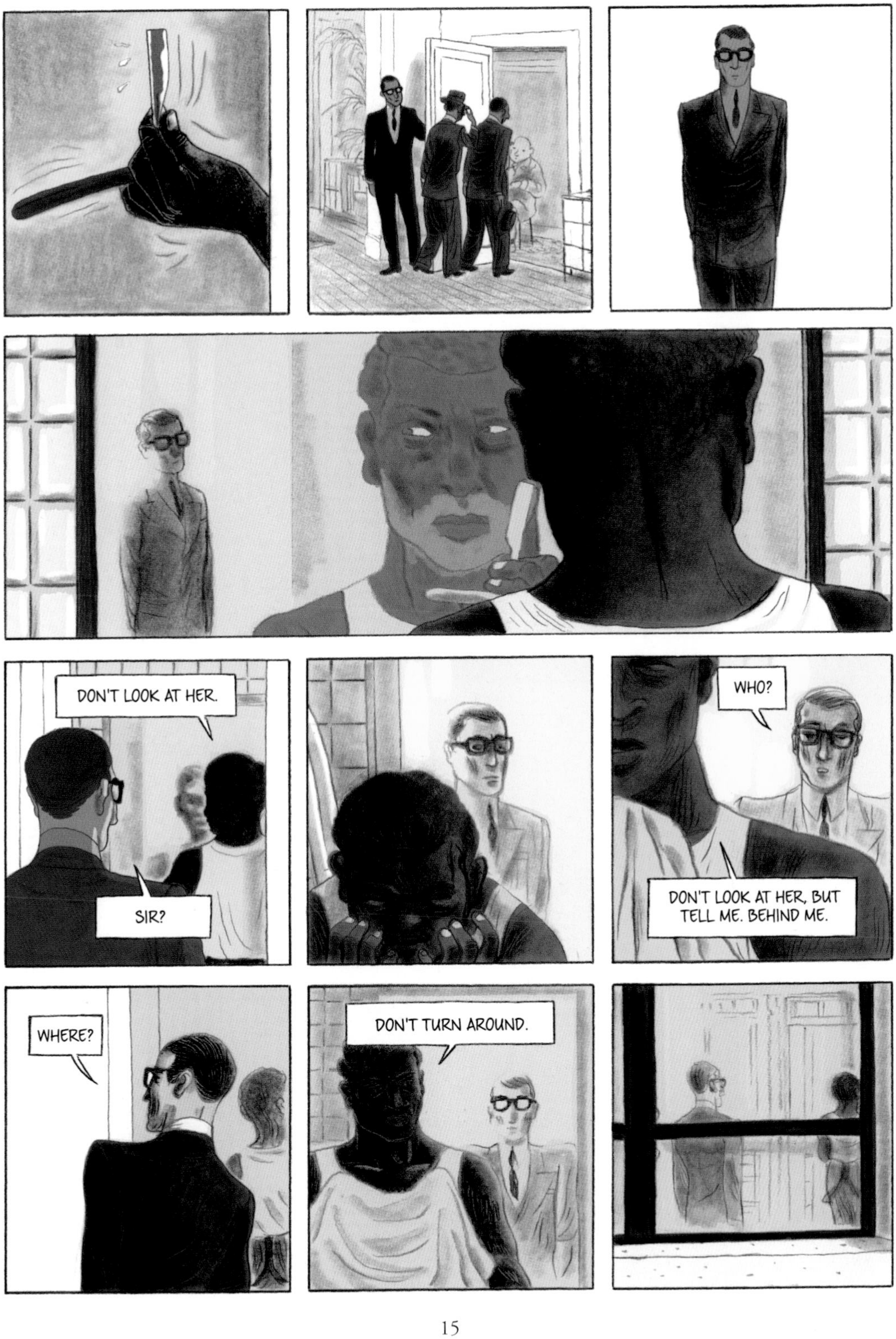
DON'T LOOK AT HER.
SIR?
WHO?
DON'T LOOK AT HER, BUT TELL ME. BEHIND ME.
WHERE?
DON'T TURN AROUND.

THERE. STAY LIKE THAT.

SEE?

AH.

THE GIRL.

SHE TOOK OVER THE CHINESE MAN'S LEASE IN JANUARY. FOSTER FOUND OUT TOO LATE TO STOP IT.

HE WANTED TO LEASE THE ROOFTOP IN YOUR NAME AND CLEAR IT ALL OUT. BUT HE WAS TOO LATE. AND HE'S ALLERGIC.

WHO?

FOSTER. THE BEES. HE'S ALLERGIC. SWELLS UP. SINCE YOU DON'T LIKE PEOPLE LOOK-ING INTO YOUR WINDOWS, HE WANTED TO CLEAR IT ALL OUT.

FOSTER?

YOUR ACCOUNTANT.

I KNOW. SHOW HIM UP.

AND BILLIE?

AT THE PARK. SHE FOUND A TOAD. GAVE IT A PAIR OF ANGEL WINGS.

IT'S ABOUT THE BEEHIVES, MR. FOSTER. I'M NOT SURE WHAT, EXACTLY.

LET ME EXPLAIN SOMETHING, MR. DAY.

CHANDLER KEPT SAYING HE'D TALK TO THE CHINESE MAN FOR TWO YEARS. BUT WE CAN FIX THIS. THE GIRL LIVES IN BROOKLYN. I HAD HER FOLLOWED.

SHE'S GOT NO ONE. NO HUSBAND. NO FAMILY. SHE'S ALL ALONE. I CAN SEND CHANDLER OVER. BURN IT ALL DOWN.

YOU'RE THE ACCOUNTANT?

ANSWER ME.

YES.

THEN WHY CONCERN YOUR-SELF WITH THE REST? BEES, NEIGHBORS, BROOKLYN GIRLS? CHINESE MEN?

IT'S LIKE THAT OTHER MAN, TALKING ABOUT HIS SISTER.

MAKE ANOTHER MOVE AGAINST THOSE HIVES, PEEK OUT THAT WINDOW AGAIN--JUST ONE MORE TIME, FOSTER, EVEN TO CHECK THE WEATHER...

AND IT'LL BE MRS. FOSTER WHO HAS NO ONE.

NOTHING.

NO FAMILY. JUST SOME OLD MAID AUNTS IN DUBLIN, MAYBE.

CORK.

EXCUSE ME?

AUNTS. IN CORK.

19

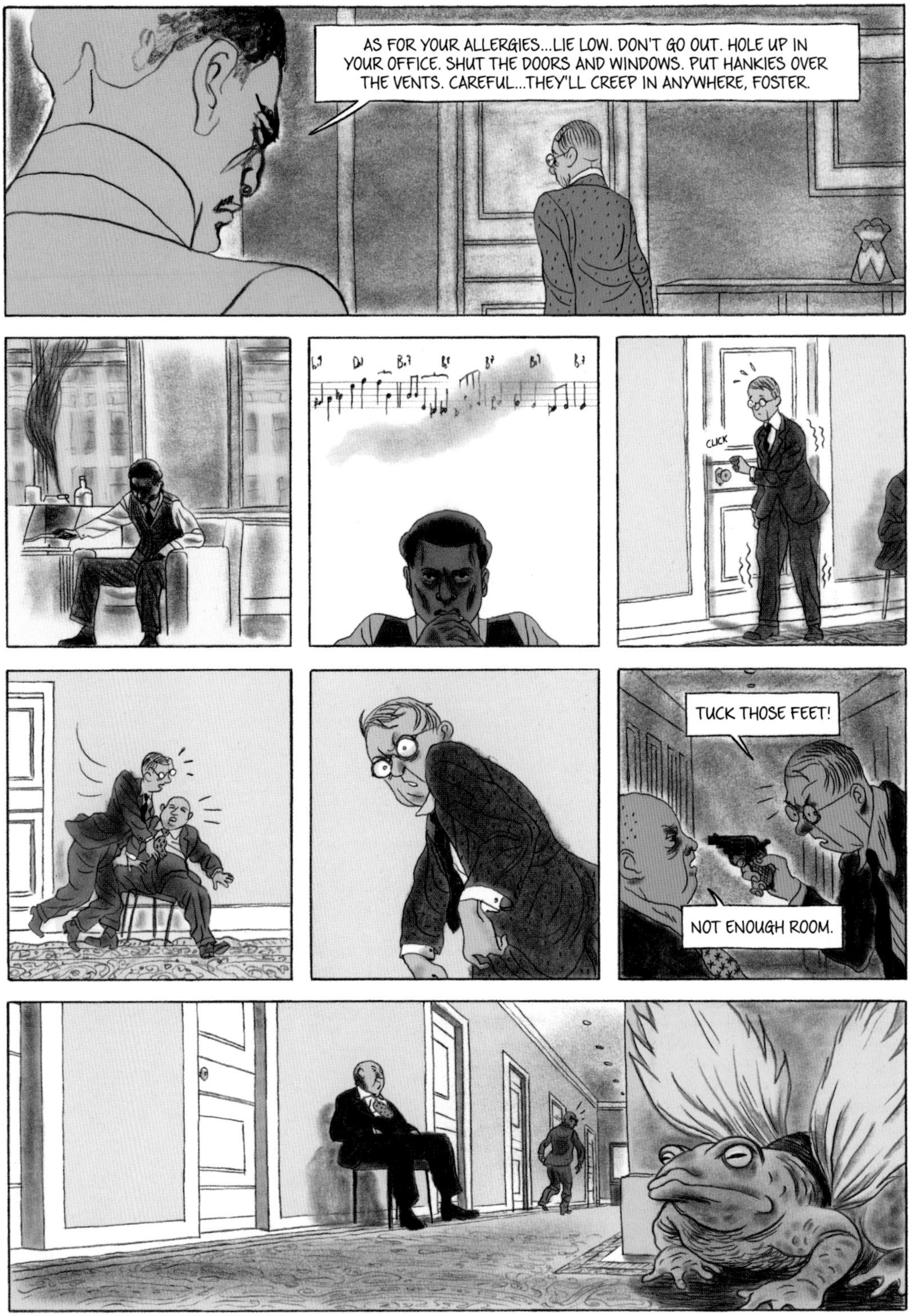
AS FOR YOUR ALLERGIES...LIE LOW. DON'T GO OUT. HOLE UP IN YOUR OFFICE. SHUT THE DOORS AND WINDOWS. PUT HANKIES OVER THE VENTS. CAREFUL...THEY'LL CREEP IN ANYWHERE, FOSTER.
CLICK
TUCK THOSE FEET!
NOT ENOUGH ROOM.

Facing a string of windows glowing like fireflies, I look for consolation.

At first, I thought I'd never be able to savor anything again. I'd lost it all. I had nothing left. Not even the memory of love.

Two years ago...
New York, march 1952

He'd shattered everything those last few years. Then he died.

YOU DON'T HAVE TO DO THIS...

He even ruined our memories.

YOU DON'T HAVE TO LOOK AT HIS FACE.

I WANT TO SEE HIM.

WE FOUND HIS OLD ARMY TAGS ON HIM. POSITIVE I.D. J.S. WHITMAN. PLEASE DON'T LIFT--

True, I didn't need to see his face. I could have described every blemish on his skin. I could have drawn his hands. Or the moles that made the big dipper on his back.

IT WAS THE WINDSHIELD. ON THE CHEVROLET. IT WAS AN ACCIDENT.

I could have drawn his every last finger.

Paris. september 1945

IS HE STILL THERE?

YES. IN FRONT OF THE DRESSING ROOM, BY THE COATS.

WHAT'S HE WANT WITH ME?

NO IDEA.

SURE YOU WON'T TAKE HIM OFF MY HANDS?

I WALKED RIGHT BY HIM THREE TIMES, CHANGING. HE'S GOT NO USE FOR ME, EVEN TOPLESS.

BUT I DON'T SPEAK ENGLISH!

THAT'S WHAT YOU TOLD HIM LAST NIGHT. FIND ANOTHER EXCUSE. G'NIGHT!

MADEMOISELLE...

THERE'S SOMEONE WAITING IN THE HALL-WAY. A BOY IN UNIFORM.

I KNOW, MONSIEUR LE DIRECTEUR.

I WATCHED YOU ON STAGE TONIGHT, MADEMOISELLE.

THANK YOU, MON-SIEUR LE DIRECTEUR.

YOU'VE ONLY ONE ADMIRER. ENJOY IT WHILE IT LASTS. SOON THEY'LL BE TRAMPLING BOUQUETS TO GET TO YOUR DRESSING ROOM. FLOWERS UP TO YOUR EARS.

24

JEREMIAH.

JEREMIAH.

JEREMIAH.

MADELEINE.

MADELEINE.

MADELEINE COME SOON.

MADELEINE VERY COQUETTE.

CROCKET?

COQUETTE.

CROCKET.

MADELEINE VERY LUCKY.

JEREMIAH LUCKY.

C'MON! DON'T BE SCARED.

THE AMERICAN.

JEREMIAH!

SO WHAT DO YOU THINK?

HE KICKED OUT THE GERMANS, BUT LOOK AT HIM, FACED WITH THREE INSECTS!

YOU'RE JEALOUS.

ME?

HAVE YOU SEEN HIS HANDS? HAVE YOU SEEN WHAT THEY'RE LIKE? JEREMIAH! COME.

WHAT IS "POOL MOO YEAH"?

POULE MOUILÉE. IT MEANS SCAREDY-CAT.

MY LITTLE GIRL, THIS IS THE END OF THE WORLD...

TASTE. IT'S HONEY.

HONEY.

The first time, he tasted like honey.

27

New York. 1954

WHERE IS IT?

SHADDUP.

IT COULDNA GOT OUT.

QUIT WRIGGLING.

HEAR THAT?

WHO CARES?

IT'S IN THE TRUNK. LISTEN, IT'S LOCKED IN THE TRUNK.

SHADDUP. QUIT TALKIN' LIKE THAT.

THE PARK!

LOOK. IT'S THAT LITTLE GIRL AGAIN. DON'T MOVE.

SHIT, IT'S IN MY PANTS.

SHADDUP, KLEBER.

THE BEE. IT'S IN MY PANTS. I GOTTA GET OUT.

YOU MOVE, I'LL SHOOT YOU.

I'M OUT.

I'LL SHOOT.

POLICE! POLICE!

DROP IT.

FORGIVE THEM, DETECTIVE. THEY'RE WATCHING THE CHILD.

WHAT'S THE MATTER WITH THE GIRL?

SHE LOCKED HERSELF IN THE PARK.

I'M TAKING YOU ALL IN!

THAT'S POINTLESS. YOU'D BE WASTING YOUR TIME. THEY'VE BROKEN NO LAWS. THEY'RE BODYGUARDS FOR THE DAY FAMILY.

SO WHY'D THE KID RUN OFF?

SHE LOST HER TOAD.

?

FETCH ANOTHER KEY TO THE PARK.

BETWEEN MY LEGS, DETECTIVE! I FEEL IT BETWEEN MY LEGS!

EVERYONE SHUT UP!

I observe humanity as I would a hive, with its mysteries and limitations.

I float above the swarm.

I'M NOT FORGIVING YOU, KLEBER. I SPENT CHRISTMAS AND EASTER IN THIS CLUNKER. I GOT SORES FROM SITTIN' ON THIS SEAT. FIRST TIME IN TEN MONTHS SOMETHING HAPPENS, AND YOU MUCK IT ALL UP. WE COULDA HAD HIM, KLEBER.

THERE WAS A BEE IN MY DRAWERS, BOSS--

SHUT YER GODDAMNED MOUTH WITH THAT BEE IN IT, KLEBER. I'LL KILL YA.

WILL I EVER GET TO CUFF GEORGE DAY?

Sometimes, the wind rises, like at sea.

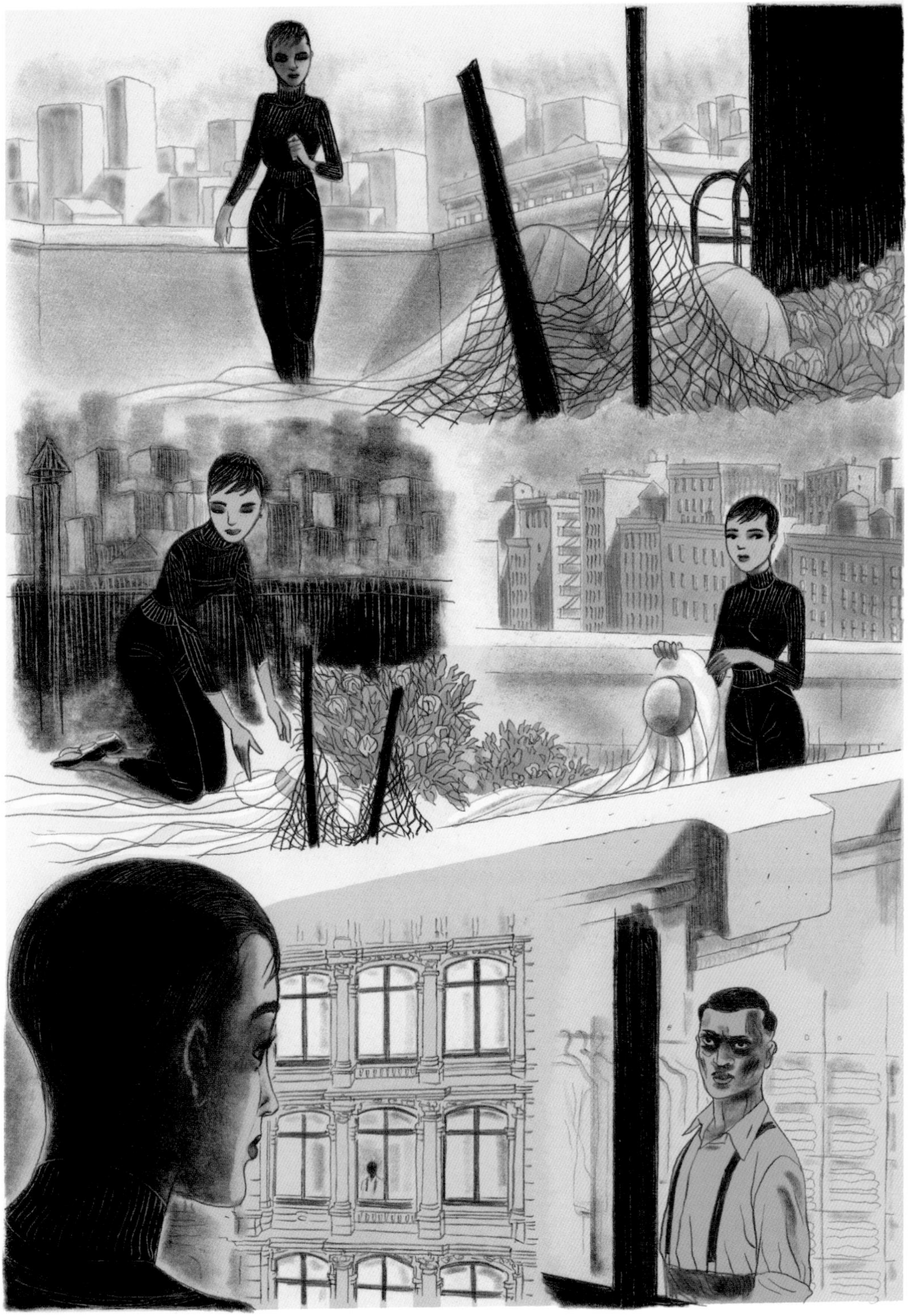

THE CHAUFFEUR'S INFORMED US THE CAR IS READY.

MISS BILLIE RAN AWAY, BUT WE FOUND HER. SHE HAD ANOTHER PARK KEY HIDDEN.

HOW MANY IS THAT?

SEVENTEEN KEYS.

SEVENTEEN?

SEVENTEEN THIS YEAR. MR. TOWNSEND, THE CO-OP PRESIDENT, SAYS HIS DOG DUG UP SIX. HE WANTS TO BAN MISS BILLIE FROM THE PARK.

TELL HIM TO GO RIGHT AHEAD, AND SOON HIS DOG'LL BE DIGGING UP ITS OWN MASTER'S BONES.

WHY WON'T SHE TALK TO ME, BRETT? WHY WON'T SHE ANSWER ME?

BILLIE?

MY CAR'S WAITING. WHEN I DON'T SAY ANYTHING, IT'S BECAUSE I DON'T KNOW.

BUT I CAN'T LIVE WITHOUT YOU, BILLIE.

35

Sundays at eleven, he goes out.

For a long time, I had no idea what he did on Sundays.

I'd picture mistresses. Country houses.

Then I'd think about his wife. How had she flown off?

She must've been pale and blonde, because the little girl's skin was barely darker than wild honey.

Paris. september 1946

LUMBAGO I'D UNDERSTAND, BUT A PETTY OFFICER!

I'D RATHER IT WERE A SPRAIN.

IF YOU'D JUST WAITED A FEW YEARS, MADEMOISELLE, I'D HAVE LET YOU LEAVE WITH ANY AMERICAN YOU LIKED.

IT MIGHT EVEN BE THE BEST ROLE YOU COULD HOPE FOR, AT THIRTY-FIVE. BUT AT YOUR AGE, WITH YOUR GIFTS AND MOREOVER, YOUR PROMISE, I MUST SAY THAT I CANNOT GIVE YOU MY BLESSING.

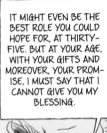

I'M SORRY.

YOU SAY THAT, BUT I SEE YOUR LIPS ALREADY QUIVERING FOR HIS MUSTACHE.

HE DOESN'T HAVE A MUSTACHE

MY POOR CHILD, THIS WILL DO YOU NO GOOD. AND YOUR GRANDFATHER?

HE SAYS HE'S HAPPY FOR ME.

AND YOU BELIEVE HIM, OF COURSE.

MADEMOISELLE, I LACK BOTH THE CHAINS AND THE CHARMS TO HOLD YOU. BUT FORGIVE ME FOR NOT SAYING FAREWELL. I ALSO LACK THE STRENGTH. GO IF YOU WISH. LEAVE US TO OUR WORK.

RIP

I won't say I didn't cry.

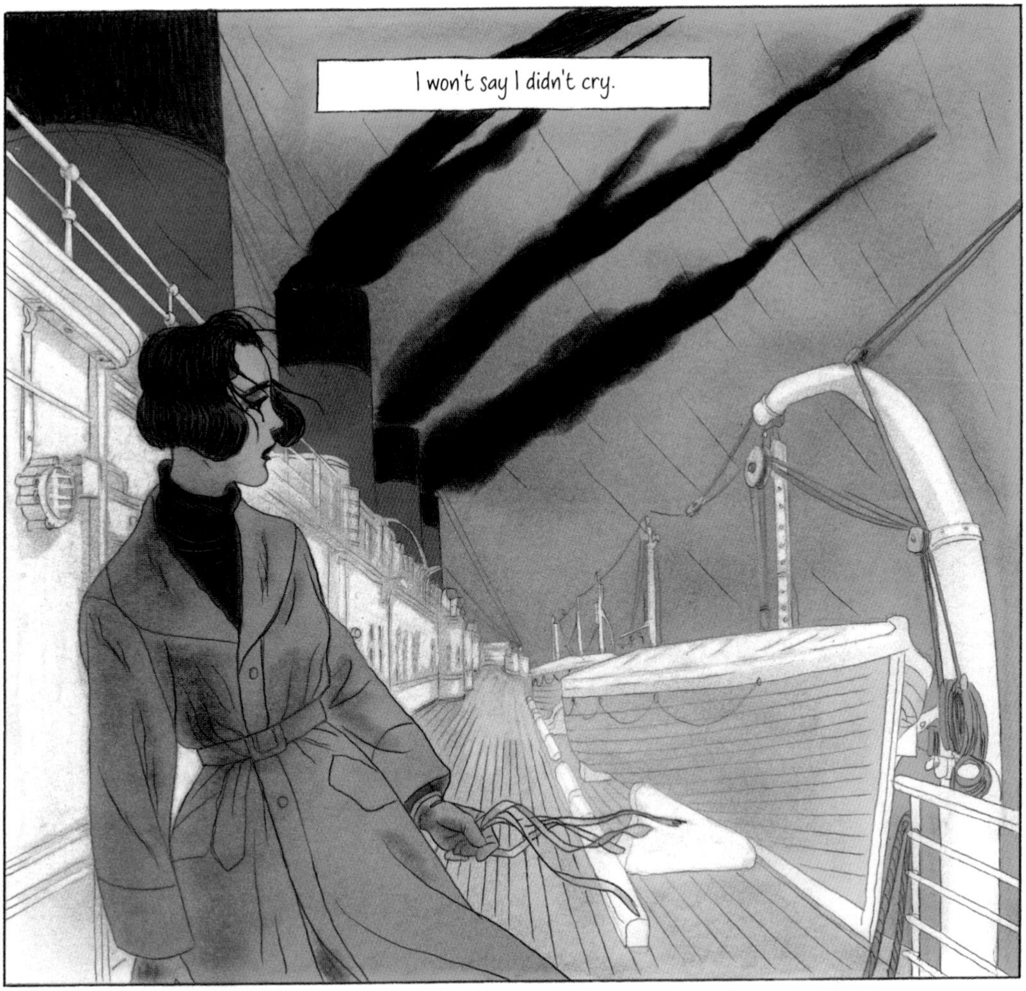
I won't say I didn't cry.

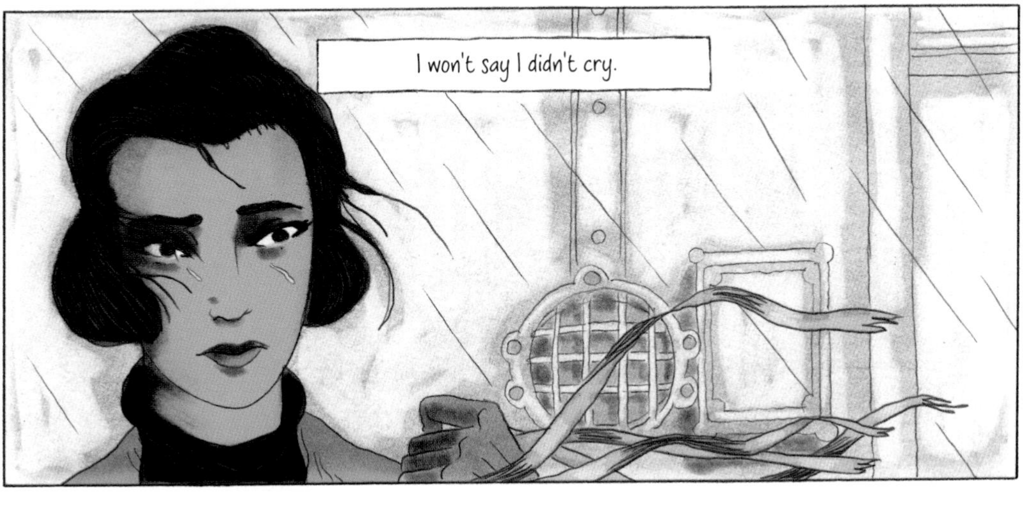
I won't say I didn't cry.

But still, there were wonderful mornings...

MADELEINE! WAKE UP!

...of consolation.

HE'S SELLING US ONE CLUB BUT KEEPING TWO, AND TAKING THE CLIENTELE WITH HIM. FOSTER'S ANNOYED.

FOSTER?

YOUR ACCOUNTANT.

WHAT'S FOSTER'S PROBLEM NOW?

HE AND BLUMENFELD AND TWO OTHERS WENT TO SEE THE MAN. TEETH WERE BROKEN.

I ASKED FOSTER TO DO SOMETHING. I THOUGHT HE WAS ALLERGIC.

WHAT?

WE BUY THE CLUB AND SAY THANKS. THAT'S ALL. PAY AND SAY THANKS. GOT IT? AND I WANT TO KNOW WHENEVER FOSTER LEAVES HIS CHAIR--EVEN TO PISS.

"THERE IS, IN THE NATURE OF THE BEE, A STRANGE DUALITY..."

WE'RE NOT STAYING ANOTHER WINTER?

BORED WITH ME? TAKE UP KNITTING.

I'M NOT BORED, I'M JUST COLD.

EVEN MORE REASON TO KNIT. LOOK, IT'S SUNDAY. HE'S GOING FOR A RIDE.

WE WON'T FIND ANYTHING, DETECTIVE. CUFF 'IM FIRST AND SEARCH LATER.

TRIED THAT ALREADY. HE'S GOT TWELVE LAWYERS WHO'D ROB US BLIND. McADAM GOT HAD THAT WAY.

WHO?

SEE? NO ONE EVEN REMEMBERS HIS NAME. NEW YORK CITY CHIEF OF POLICE. NOW HE RAISES HENS AND RABBITS AT HIS PARENTS' PLACE NEAR LAKE MICHIGAN.

One Sunday, I followed him.

I hadn't planned to.

I'M ONLY DOING THIS BE-
CAUSE YOU DON'T LOOK
LIKE A GANGSTER.

But when I saw him leave
that day, I followed.

HE CHEATIN' ON YA? SOMETHIN' LIKE
THAT, RIGHT? AND THE OTHER CAR,
THE BLACK ONE? THE MISTRESS'S
HUSBAND, RIGHT?

FOLLOW THEM.

I SEEN IT ALL, HEH.
COMES WITH THE JOB.
AND THE FLOWERS?

Things like this don't
happen in real life.

We drove north for two hours, leaving the city behind.

We drove through the woods.

WHAT IF THAT GUY IS JUST GOIN' BEAVER HUNTING? WOMEN ALWAYS BELIEVE THE WORST. YOU OKAY? DREAMIN'?

New York, 1947

For two years, my happiness was complete. We lived off of Jeremiah's savings as a soldier, in a little apartment on the edge of Harlem.

Children taught me their language.

I spoke like a guttersnipe.

Jeremiah would bring me surprises.

"YOU WROTE THAT YOU WERE DIS-APPOINTED I'M NOT DANCING HERE. WHY? EVERY DAY FEELS LIKE A DANCE. MY LIFE IS MY DANCE, GRANDFATHER..."

"WHEN WILL YOU COME TO SEE US? THE LIBERTY HAS CROSSINGS FOR $300. I PUT SOME MONEY ASIDE IN THE SUGAR BOX EVERY MONTH."

I THOUGHT ABOUT THE NAVY. MY OLD MAN WANTED ME TO JOIN THE NAVY.

HOW 'BOUT YOU, DETECTIVE? THEY SAY YOU TRIED TO BE IN MOVIES.

THEY SAY A LOT OF THINGS.

SO IT'S TRUE?

THEY EVEN SAY I SHOT A GUY FOR ASKING ME A STUPID QUESTION.

LOOKS LIKE WE'RE HERE.

THIS IS NO PLACE TO HUNT BEAVERS, I'LL TELL YA.

LEMME JUST SEE WHERE WE ARE.

WAIT.

One day, Jeremiah left me alone in a car for hours. Now I know everything changed that night.

Life took a different turn.

His army pay had run out a year ago. I worked nights ironing in the laundry at the Claridge Hotel. I didn't know what Jeremiah did with his nights.

He'd picked me up after my shift, driving a car that wasn't his. He was supposed to drop off a package at a bar on 7th Street.

He did odd jobs. Said he was doing people favors.

He was still gone when I woke. He'd told me to stay put.

48

I'll never know if I dreamed that part.

WHAT WERE YOU DOING?

THE DISHES.

Some memories are like nightmares.

WHO'S THAT?

BUT YOUR HAT?

LET'S GO. I DON'T LIKE THIS.

WHERE ARE WE?

GUESS.

Hudson River State Hospital
POUGHKEEPSIE N.Y.

A MADHOUSE.

I'd pictured country houses with mistresses rolled up in furs by a fire, but he'd gone to see someone at a madhouse.

RIBBIT.

C'MERE, EDWARD. C'MERE.

CROA

BONK!

CLICK

YOU PLAYING MARBLES?

JUST PASSING BY. AM I INTERRUPTING?

I KNOW YOU'VE BEEN SAYING THINGS ABOUT ME TO THE BOSS. JUST BECAUSE HE'S GOT YOU CLEANING UP HIS SHIT DOESN'T MAKE YOU HIS NANNY.

YOU'RE MISTAKEN, MR. FOSTER.

I'VE GOT A BRIEFCASE FULL OF DIRT ON YOU, BRETT. WHAT WERE YOU DOING HERE?

EMPTYING THE TRASH.

GOOD NIGHT, MR. FOSTER.

I HAVE EDWARD, MISS BILLIE.

HE'S LOST HIS WINGS.

I THINK WE'LL HAVE TO RELEASE HIM IN THE PARK. HE TOLD ME HE MISSES HIS FAMILY.

HE'S A TOAD. HE DOESN'T TALK ABOUT HIS FAMILY.

OH?

HE NEVER TALKS.

I THINK HE'S JUST BEING CONSIDERATE. HE DOESN'T WANT TO MAKE YOU SAD.

SLEEP WELL, MISS BILLIE. YOUR FATHER WILL BE HOME SOON.

WHAT FATHER?

I only go up once all winter.

They're sleeping.

I watch those warm little boxes way up high.

They keep the hives as warm as a human body. Warm as a bed in the morning.

The bees recognize my voice in their long night. I whisper to them.

Christmas 1949

I felt him growing distant.

One night near Christmas, he forgot to come for me.

NO, I'M WAIT-ING FOR MY HUSBAND.

IT'S COLD OUT. WOULD YOU LIKE TO WAIT IN MY ROOM?

THANKS. I'M JUST FINE IN MY COAT, SEE?

YOU WON'T NEED IT UP THERE.

LEAVE ME ALONE. PLEASE.

THAT LAUNDRY GIRL PICKING UP SOME OVER-TIME WITH GUESTS?

53

THE SALVATION ARMY

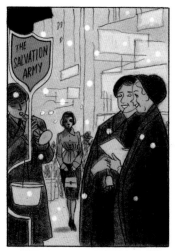

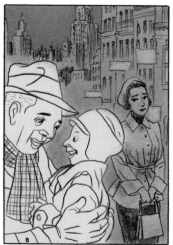

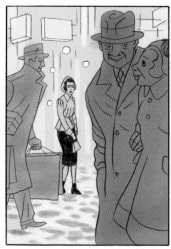

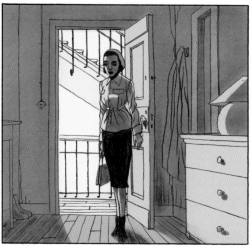

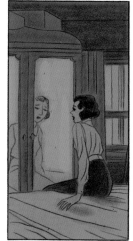

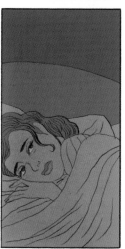

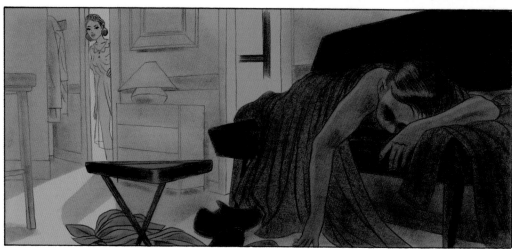

THEY ALL WANT KIDS TO GIVE 'EM SOME- THING TO HOLD.

I DIDN'T SAY ANYTHING.

YOU USUALLY DO.

I BROUGHT UP CHRISTMAS.

SAME DIFFERENCE.

I WAITED FOR YOU. PEOPLE THOUGHT I WAS A WHORE.

DON'T SAY THAT WORD. I CAN'T LISTEN TO MY WIFE SAY THAT WORD.

55

WHORE. YOU DON'T LIKE IT WHEN YOUR WIFE SAYS IT, BUT YOU'RE FINE SPENDING THE NIGHT WITH ONE.

SHUT UP, MADELEINE. I COULD KILL YOU WHEN YOU TALK LIKE THAT.

The next three days, he kept looking for something. Something he'd lost.

He wouldn't say what it was.

Much later, when I left for Brooklyn and he'd been dead for months, I searched for somewhere warm and dry to keep the gun.

In the wintertime, the hive is a kingdom aslumber.

Like birds in the sky, I was waiting for spring.

HOW MANY YEARS YOU BEEN MARRIED, DETECTIVE?

FOURTEEN.

AND YOU DON'T MISS 'EM?

WHAT?

THE OTHERS. ALL THE OTHERS. LOOK. THEY'RE EVERYWHERE.

MA'AM? DE-
TECTIVE
ANGELINO.

YES?

DO YOU KNOW
MR. DAY?

WHO?

GEORGE DAY. INVESTI-
GATIN' THE NEIGH-
BORHOOD.

NO.

LIVES TWO BUILDINGS
DOWN. YOU LIVE HERE
TOO?

I WORK HERE. I
LIVE ELSEWHERE.

LINE OF WORK?

HONEY. I WORK
WITH HONEY.
EXCUSE ME. I'M
EXPECTED.

HONEY. YOU BE-
LIEVE THAT?

WHAT?

WORKS IN HONEY.

YOU ACCOST
HER LIKE
THAT...

I SEEN HER
AROUND HERE
LOTS.

YOU GOT A GOOD EYE, BOSS.

HONEY. WHAT THE
HECK'S THAT MEAN?

He left nothing of himself behind.
No letters. No photos. Not even an old shirt that smelled like him.

He'd sold the ribbons from my ballet slippers. The ones with the gold thread. He left me with nothing.

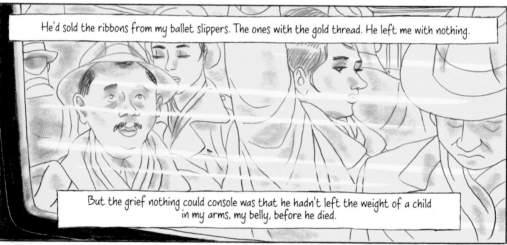

But the grief nothing could console was that he hadn't left the weight of a child in my arms, my belly, before he died.

A little orphan, that tiny weight.

He left nothing of himself behind.

"HERE, THEY HAVE SHAKEN OFF THE TORPOR OF WINTER.

"THEN SPRING INVADES THE EARTH..."

WORD IS YOU DON'T WANT ME ANYMORE.

S'WHAT I HEAR. SO I JOINED UP WITH LEE GORDON'S BOXERS.

WHO?

LEE GORDON.

I'M ASKING WHO TOLD YOU THAT?

WHAT?

THAT I DON'T WANT YOU ANYMORE.

FOSTER.

FOSTER?

YEAH, FOSTER.

BRETT?

SIR?

TELL FOSTER TO COME UP.

IT'S SUNDAY, SIR. YOUR CAR'S WAITING.

CLAK

GET ME FOSTER!

HE'S LATE. IT'S NOT LIKE HIM.

DON'T GET MY HOPES UP, DETECTIVE.

HE GONNA MISS HIS SUNDAY DATE?

IF HE SPARED US THE FIVE HOUR DRIVE, I--

HOLD ON.

WHAT?

LOOK.

THIS TIME, IT'S LOVE.

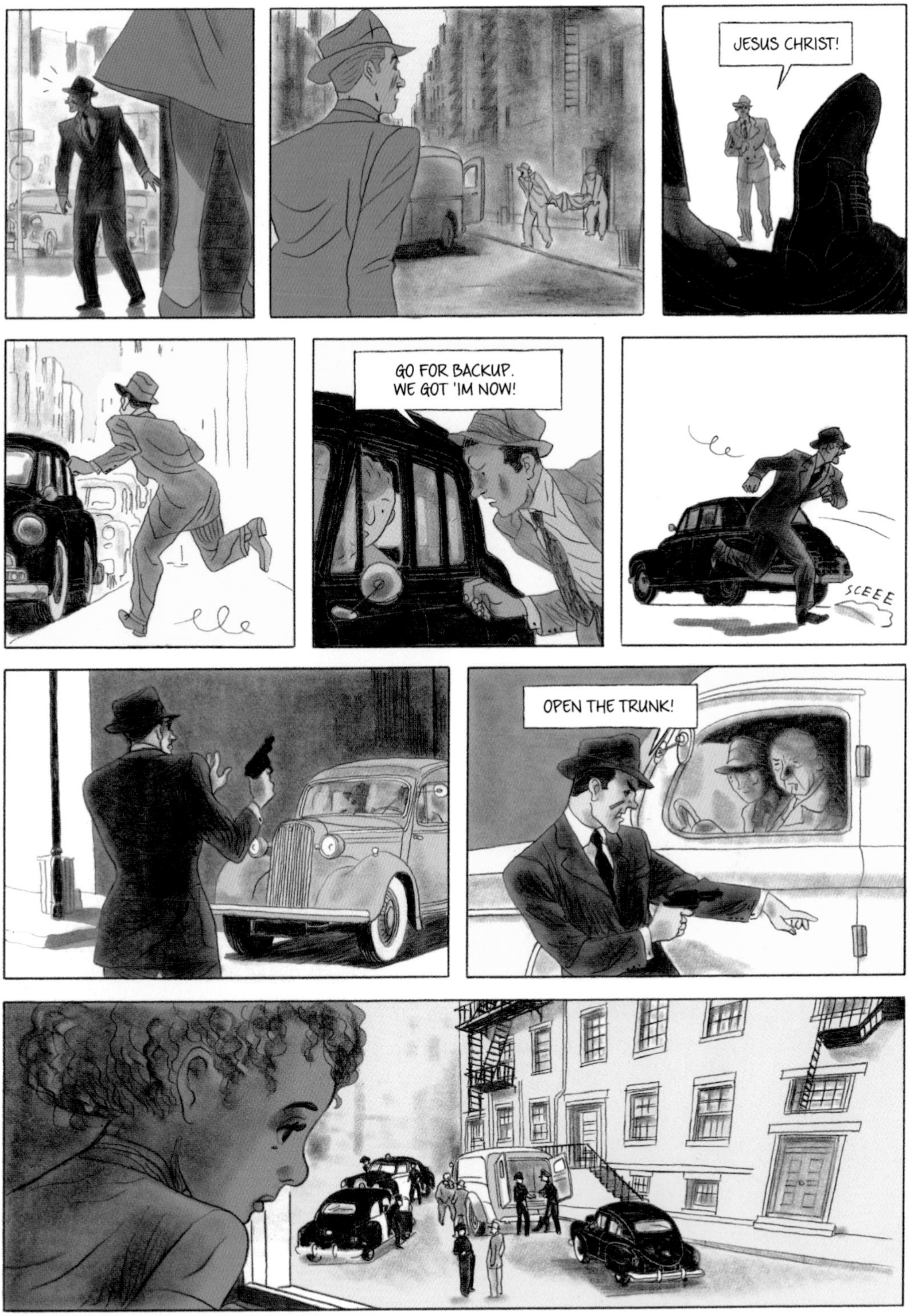
JESUS CHRIST!
GO FOR BACKUP.
WE GOT 'IM NOW!
SCEEE
OPEN THE TRUNK!

JUST IN TIME.

MR. DAY WOULD LIKE TO BUY YOU A DRINK, DETECTIVE.

NOTHIN' DOIN'! I'M BUSTIN' UP THE JOINT, I'M BUYIN'!

HE ASKED FIRST. BY JUST A HAIR.

NO! THIS IS A RAID!

AN INVITATION.

WHO WAS THAT GUY? WHAT DID YOU DO TO HIM?

TRY SOME.

I ASKED YOU A QUESTION.

IT'S GLENFARCLAS. AS OLD AS YOUR SON.

LUCKY FOR YOU THAT GUY'S ALIVE! HE'S--HOW DO YOU KNOW MY SON'S AGE?

HAVE A SIP. YOU'LL LOVE IT.

YOU THREATENING MY FAMILY?

YOU'RE A FUNNY MAN, DETECTIVE. YOU CAN COMB THROUGH MY GARBAGE, BUT I'M NOT ALLOWED TO KNOW YOU HAVE A SON? HIS NAME'S FOSTER.

NO. PETER.

I'M NOT TALKING ABOUT YOUR SON. STOP SHARING YOUR PRIVATE LIFE. I'M TALKING ABOUT THE MAN YOU FOUND DOWN BELOW.

YOU KNOW HIM?

HE'S MY ACCOUNTANT.

DID YOU DO THAT TO HIM?

DO YOU THINK I'D TOUCH A HAIR ON HIS HEAD WHEN I CAN'T EVEN COUNT?

SEE THE COLOR OF MY SKIN? IT'S BLACK. I NEVER WENT TO SCHOOL. I MANAGE BOXING MATCHES AND MUSIC CLUBS.

I'M WARNING YOU, DAY. YOU CAN'T HIDE A THING. MY MEN ARE EXAMINING HIM.

THEY'LL BE THE DEATH OF HIM, IF THEY DON'T GET HIM HELP SOON.

WHAT?

FOSTER IS ALLERGIC.

ALLERGIC?

TO BEES. HE'D TELL YOU HIMSELF, BUT HIS TONGUE'S SWOLLEN LIKE A CALF'S. HE JUST GOT STUNG IN THE MOUTH. HE'S GOING TO DIE ON YOUR WATCH, AND YOU'LL OWE HIS WIFE A PEN-SION, DETECTIVE ANGELINO. I'VE DONE ALL I CAN.

WHERE IS MY CAR?

I SENT IT BACK TO THE GARAGE. THE POLICE DON'T WANT YOU LEAVING TODAY.

I NEVER ASKED YOU TO. CALL IT OVER AGAIN.

I THINK YOU SHOULD STAY IN, MR. DAY.

OUT OF MY WAY!

MR. DAY, I KNOW...BILLIE'S MOTHER WOULD WANT YOU TO STAY.

IF THEY EVER AR- REST YOU ONE DAY...

DON'T LIE TO ME LIKE ALL THE OTHERS. DON'T MAKE ME THINK SHE NEEDS ME.

HUDSON RIVER STATE HOSPITAL

HE DIDN'T GIVE YOU A NOTE?

NO.

IT'S SUNDAY. WE WERE EXPECTING HIM. HE ALWAYS COMES. THIS IS A FIRST.

YES. THAT'S WHY HE SENT ME.

ARE YOU FAMILY?

NO.

HE OUGHT TO HAVE TOLD YOU THE RULES.

YES. HE TOLD ME TO INSIST.

MR. DAY HAS BEEN VERY GENEROUS TO OUR ESTABLISHMENT.

HE SAID YOU'D UNDERSTAND.

YOU'VE PUT ME IN A DIFFICULT POSITION, MISS.

I didn't even know whom I'd come to see. I just felt...drawn.

HE JUST WANTED SOME-ONE TO BE HERE.

DO YOU REALLY THINK THE PATIENT KNOWS THE DIFFERENCE?

THIS WAY.

THIS IS THE MEN'S WING. THE NICEST ONES GET TO WALK AROUND FREELY.

AND HERE ARE THE WOMEN.

GO ON IN. YOU'LL ONLY HAVE A FEW MINUTES. MRS. DAY IS VERY WEAK AND NOT ALL THERE.

LOOK AT THESE PHOTOS ALL OVER THE FLOOR. I CAN'T EVEN PICK THEM UP ANYMORE.

THEY SLIDE THEM IN UNDER THE DOOR. I'M GLAD YOU CAME. I HOPE YOU'LL FORGIVE ME FOR ALL THE PAIN I'VE CAUSED YOU. THERE MUST BE A PHOTO OF YOU. WAIT, HE SHOWED ME A PHOTO OF YOU.

WHO?

MY DAUGHTER'S FATHER. DO YOU KNOW HER? I DON'T HAVE A PHOTO OF HER. I KEEP LOOKING, BUT THEY WON'T GIVE ME ONE.

YES, I KNOW HER. SHE'S BEAUTIFUL.

MY LITTLE GIRL.

I HOPE SOMEDAY YOU'LL FORGIVE ME FOR WHAT I DID TO YOU. YOU'RE EVEN PRETTIER THAN YOU ARE IN PHOTOS. I KNOW I'M GOING TO DIE. FEEL MY HEART IN MY FINGERTIPS.

YOU'VE DONE NOTHING TO ME.

TELL THEM TO LEAVE ME ALONE. I DON'T HAVE THE STRENGTH TO PICK THEM ALL UP. I'VE SUFFERED ENOUGH.

WHERE IS THE WOMAN WHO CAME TO SEE ESTHER DAY?

SHE JUST LEFT.

I CALLED MR. DAY. HE DIDN'T SEND ANYONE.

TELL ANGELINO THAT IF ANY OF HIS MEN EVER TRY TO SEE MY WIFE AGAIN--

I'LL TELL HIM, SIR.

TELL HIM, BRETT. TELL HIM IF ANYONE TRIES EVEN ONCE...

The next day, still full of secrets from that white room, I planted my lines of cosmos.

The bees were coming back from suburban orchards full of flowering cherries.

Across the street, they'd drawn the curtains as if someone had died.

MADELEINE WHITMAN...

BIRDS THAT WE CAN'T NAB IN FLIGHT, WE TRACK TO THEIR NESTS.

AND SINCE YOU DON'T LOOK LIKE YOU'RE ABOUT TO GIVE ME ANY ANSWERS, I BROUGHT SOME OF MY OWN. MADELEINE ROSE WHITMAN, BORN IN PARIS, WIDOWED, LIVING IN BROOKLYN. YOU TOOK OVER MR. WONG'S LEASE FOR THE ROOF AND THE FIRE ESCAPE.

WHAT ARE YOU DOING HERE?

NEVER KNEW THERE WERE HIVES IN MANHATTAN.

WHERE THERE'S LIFE, THERE ARE BEES.

YOU MENTIONED HONEY BEFORE. I SAW THE HIVES. I MADE THE CONNECTION.

YOU MUST BE A DETECTIVE.

I think he realized right away I wouldn't be much use to him.

From that day on, I was to see him once a week and make a report.

He wasn't asking a favor. He was giving an order.

I would be a witness in his case. He showed me a judge's letter with my name on it.

I was the only person who could see what went on over there.

MAYBE. I'M NOT SURE. THE FAT ONE MIGHT HAVE COME YESTERDAY, BUT IN A DIFFERENT COAT.

LIKE I CARE ABOUT HIS COAT. WAS HE THERE?

NO.

HOW ABOUT THE BLOND?

WHAT'S SO FUNNY?

HIS HAIRCUT.

It was a game. I was enjoying myself again.

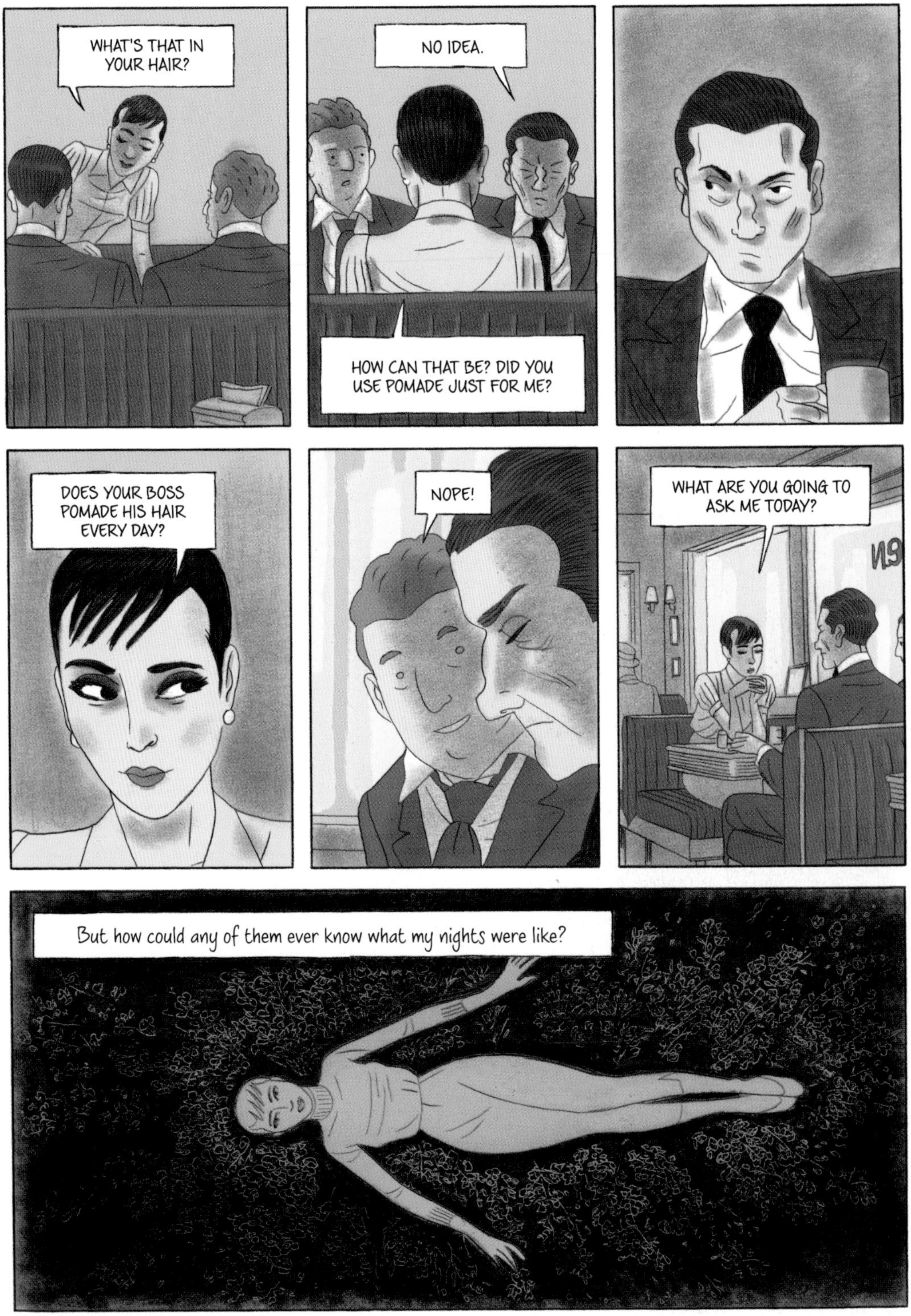

WHAT'S THAT IN YOUR HAIR?
NO IDEA.
HOW CAN THAT BE? DID YOU USE POMADE JUST FOR ME?
DOES YOUR BOSS POMADE HIS HAIR EVERY DAY?
NOPE!
WHAT ARE YOU GOING TO ASK ME TODAY?
But how could any of them ever know what my nights were like?

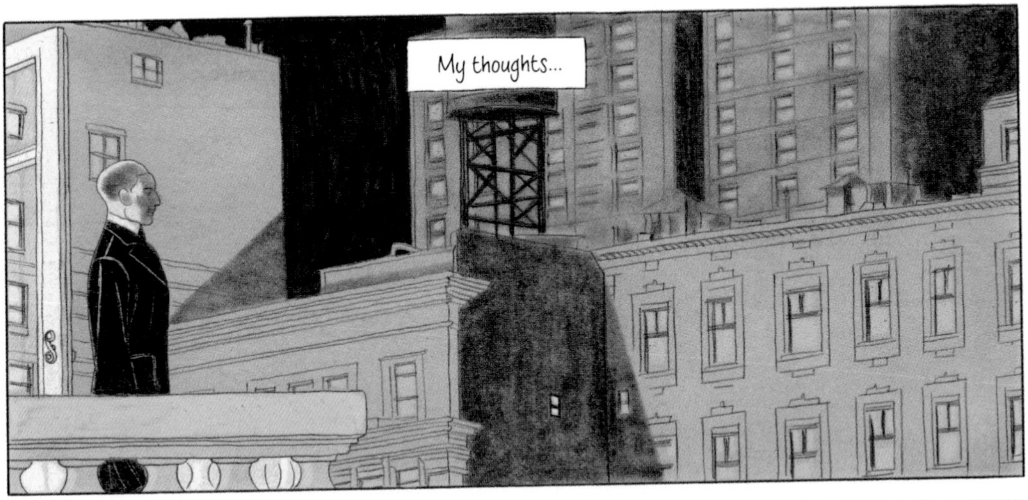
My thoughts...

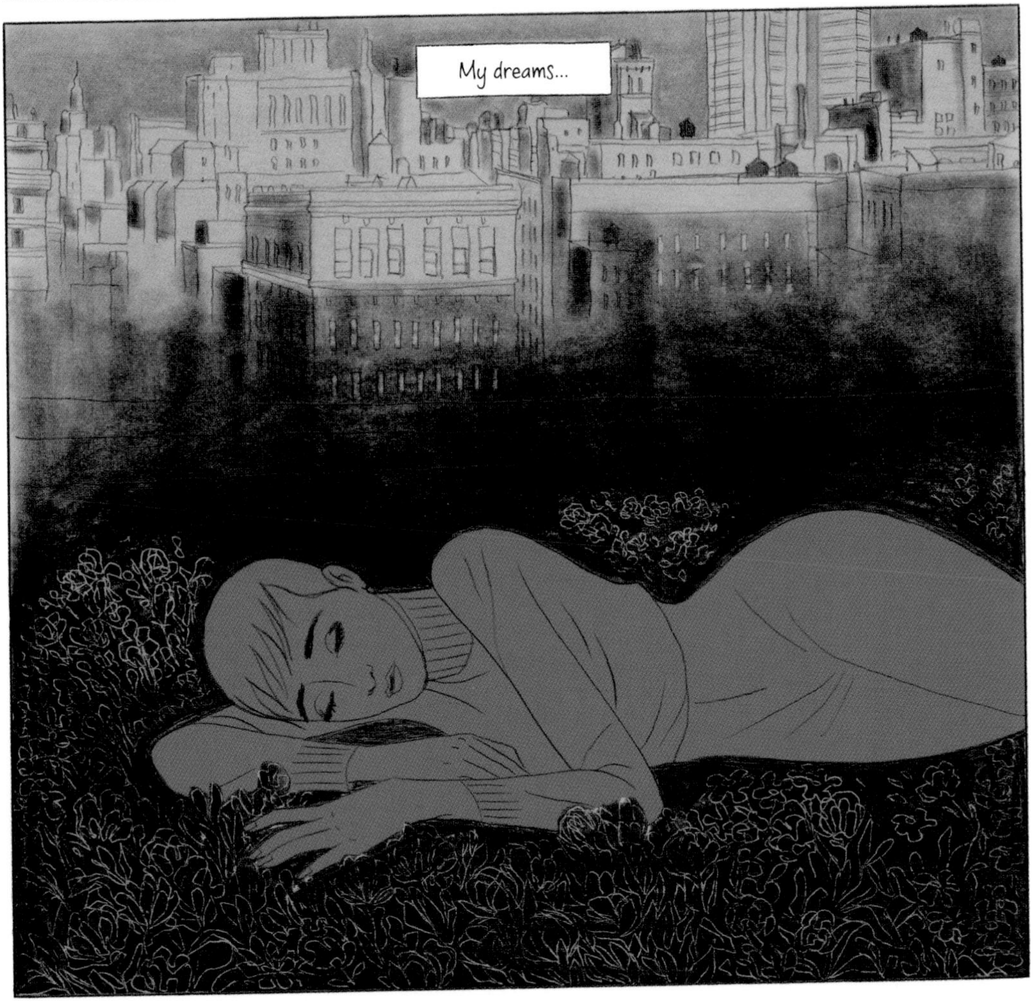
My dreams...

New York, 1952

JEREMIAH?

JEREMIAH?

JEREMIAH?

YOU'RE HOME.

I DID SOMETHING I SHOULDN'T HAVE, MADELEINE.

COME.

NO.

I KNOW YOU'RE LOST. I KNOW YOUR LIFE'S GONE CROOKED. I CAN HELP YOU START ALL OVER.

IT'S TOO LATE, MADELEINE.

I KNOW YOU LIED TO ME A THOUSAND TIMES.

YOU DON'T GET IT...

YOU'RE TIRED.

I KNOW YOU THREATENED PEOPLE. KILLED THEM.

MADELEINE...

I KNOW THERE WERE OTHER WOMEN, JEREMIAH. YOU GAVE THEM MY GOLD-THREADED RIBBONS. I KNOW.

THAT'S NOT WHAT I MEAN. I...

WE CAN START ALL OVER.

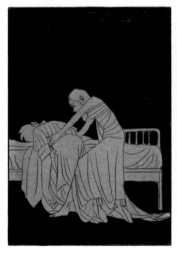

New York, 1955

FORGIVE ME, MA'AM. I WOULD'VE RUNG, BUT I DIDN'T SEE A BELL. WOULD YOU LIKE MY UMBRELLA?

NO.

I'M HERE ON BEHALF OF A NEIGHBOR.

My God.

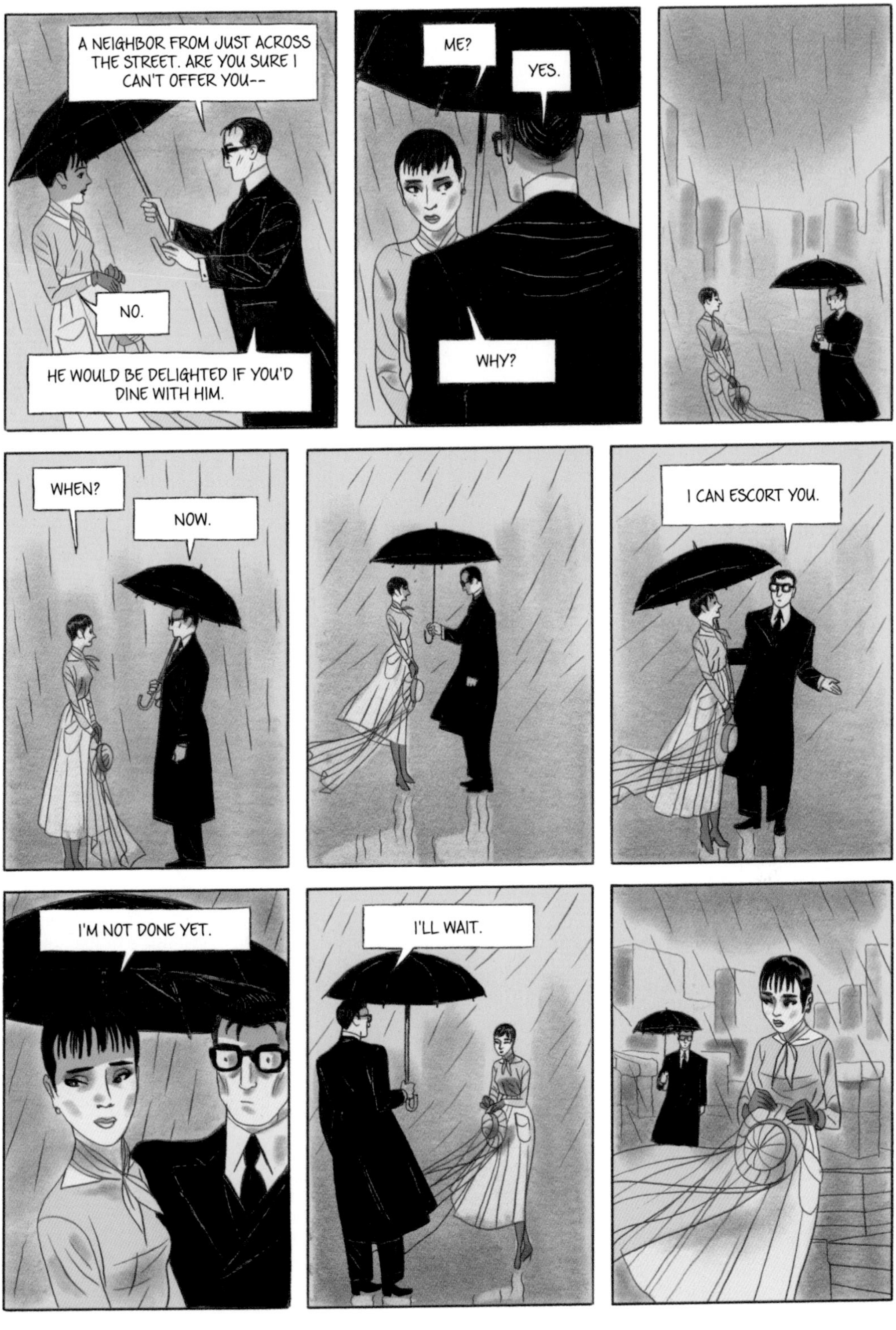
A NEIGHBOR FROM JUST ACROSS THE STREET. ARE YOU SURE I CAN'T OFFER YOU--
NO.
HE WOULD BE DELIGHTED IF YOU'D DINE WITH HIM.
ME?
YES.
WHY?
WHEN?
NOW.
I CAN ESCORT YOU.
I'M NOT DONE YET.
I'LL WAIT.

My God. What did he want? What did he know?

WOULD YOU LIKE TO CHANGE?

MY WIFE STILL HAS SOME CLOTHES HERE.

WHERE IS YOUR WIFE?

NOT HERE ANYMORE.

THANK YOU FOR COMING.

I CAME BECAUSE THE GENTLEMAN WITH THE UMBRELLA WAS NICE. IS HE DINING WITH US?

BRETT? NO.

DO YOU OFTEN INVITE PEOPLE YOU DON'T KNOW?

I HARDLY KNOW ANYONE.

CAN WE SIT CLOSER TO THE FIRE?

After that, we didn't say a word.

I think I looked normal.

But the world was burning inside me.

When it was over, I stood up.

I KNOW THE WAY.

I balled my hands up to keep them from shaking.

It was the moment I'd been waiting for.

I knew he must have sent all his men away.

Just us.

It would have all ended right there if I hadn't seen her eyes.

I'd have gotten some consolation at last.

I DON'T KNOW WHY I KEEP MEETING WITH YOU.

ME EITHER.

STILL NOTHING TO REPORT?

THAT'S THE SECOND CUP YOU'VE SPIKED.

YOU STAKING ME OUT NOW?

YOU'RE AN ODD ONE. RIGHT FROM THE START, I WONDERED WHAT IT WAS YOU WERE DOING UP THERE. WHAT ARE YOU AFTER, MADELEINE?

CONSOLATION.

WHAT?

A LITTLE SWEET-NESS. YOU DRINK TOO MUCH. YOU SAID MADELEINE, NOT MRS. WHITMAN.

HIS WIFE DIED YESTERDAY. SHE'D BEEN INTERNED FOR THREE YEARS.

HE WALKS AWAY AND LEAVES A TRAIL OF BODIES BEHIND: ALLERGIES, SUICIDES...I'M SURPRISED NO TRUCKS HAVE RUN ME OVER ON MY WAY HOME YET.

DETECTIVE--YOU OUGHTA HEAR THIS.

I'M WITH A LADY.

WE'VE GOT 'IM, DETECTIVE! SOME GUY CAME IN AND SPILLED HIS GUTS. WE'VE GOT 'IM NOW!

WHERE IS THIS GUY?

IN YOUR OFFICE. IT'S LIGHTS OUT FOR GEORGE DAY!

Coincidences are strange.

That very morning, I'd taken a queen from a hive and put her in a cage as if packing my bags.

New York, 1952

BEEN LOOKING ALL OVER FOR YOU.

MY GRAND-FATHER'S DEAD.

POOR MADE-LEINE.

STAY WITH ME TONIGHT.

TOMORROW.

STAY HOME WITH ME. PLEASE.

JEREMIAH...

WHO IS SHE? WHAT'S HER NAME?

WHO DID YOU GIVE MY GOLD-THREADED RIBBONS TO? JEREMIAH...

WHERE IS HE?

FOSTER!

WHAT IS IT THIS TIME? A SHELLFISH ALLERGY?

IT'S ALL ON THE TABLE.

I DON'T GIVE A DAMN ABOUT ANY OF THIS. THE COURTS WON'T EITHER. SO HE'S A BIG BAD WOLF WITH BIG BAD TEETH AND BIG BAD EARS. WHO CARES? I WANT A CRIME, JUST ONE LITTLE CRIME, WITH NAMES, DATES, AND PROOF!

RIIIIIP

G-GOT ONE.

PROOF.

I KILLED A MAN FOR HIM.

GIVE HIM A CIGARETTE.

IT WASN'T LIKE THE OTHER TIMES. THAT'S WHY HE NEVER FORGAVE ME. IT WASN'T LIKE THEM AT ALL.

YOU KEEP REPEATING YOUR-SELF, SO HELP ME GOD, I'LL MAKE SURE YOU SERVE TWICE AS LONG IN JAIL.

THIS GUY WAS SLEEPING WITH DAY'S WIFE. HE MADE ME KILL HIM IN FRONT OF HER.

THAT'S BETTER.

THE GUY WAS IN THE CAR WITH HER. DAY GOT HIS WIFE OUT AND WE RAN THE CHEVY INTO THE BRIDGE PILING.

TAP
TAP
TAP

HE NEVER FORGAVE ME FOR HIS WIFE GOING CRAZY. BUT I DID EXACTLY WHAT HE TOLD ME TO.

GOT A DATE?

MARCH 12, 1952.

A NAME?

TAP
TAP
TAP

WHITMAN. JEREMIAH WHITMAN.

WHO?

JEREMIAH WHITMAN.

MADELEINE...

BOSS?

MADELEINE WHITMAN. THAT'S WHY SHE'S THERE.

WHAT?

SHE'S THERE TO KILL HIM.

ARE YOU SURE, MA'AM?

YES. I'M GOING UP ALONE. DON'T NOTIFY HIM.

DO I SCARE YOU?

The element of surprise lay in walking right through the front door like everyone else.

And wearing lipstick.

For three years I'd waited for this day. I'd followed the trail of the man who'd taken mine from me.

But behind one door, someone was crying.

CAN'T SLEEP?

YOU SHOULD SLEEP.

WHAT'S YOUR NAME?

WHAT'S THAT IN YOUR HAIR?

WHO GAVE YOU THAT RIBBON?

MY MOMMY.

89

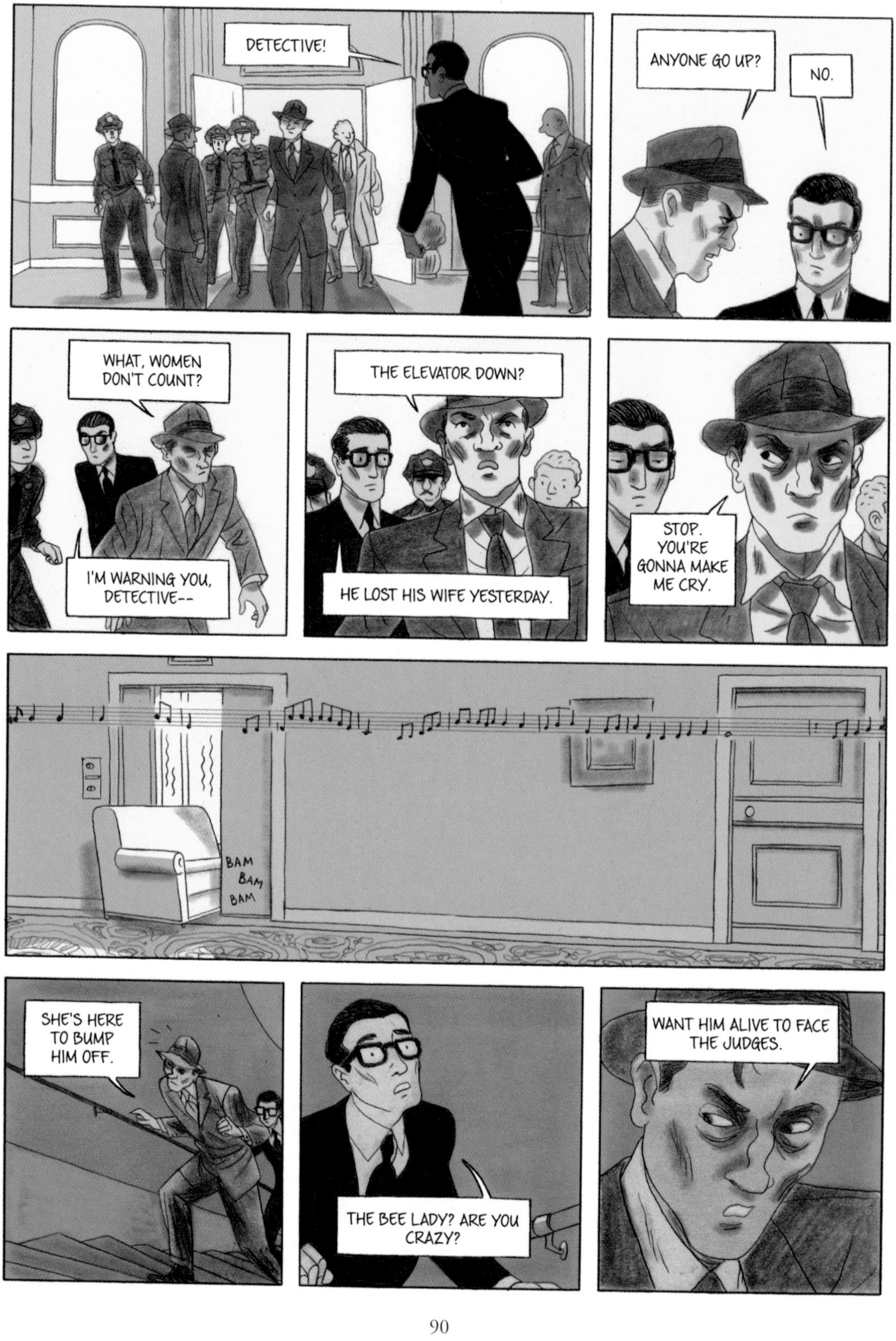
DETECTIVE!
ANYONE GO UP?
NO.
WHAT, WOMEN DON'T COUNT?
I'M WARNING YOU, DETECTIVE--
THE ELEVATOR DOWN?
HE LOST HIS WIFE YESTERDAY.
STOP. YOU'RE GONNA MAKE ME CRY.
BAM
BAM
BAM
SHE'S HERE TO BUMP HIM OFF.
THE BEE LADY? ARE YOU CRAZY?
WANT HIM ALIVE TO FACE THE JUDGES.

MR. DAY?

YES, BRETT.

DID SHE COME FOR YOU?

WHO?

I'M SORRY I LET HER UP.

WHO ARE YOU TALKING ABOUT?

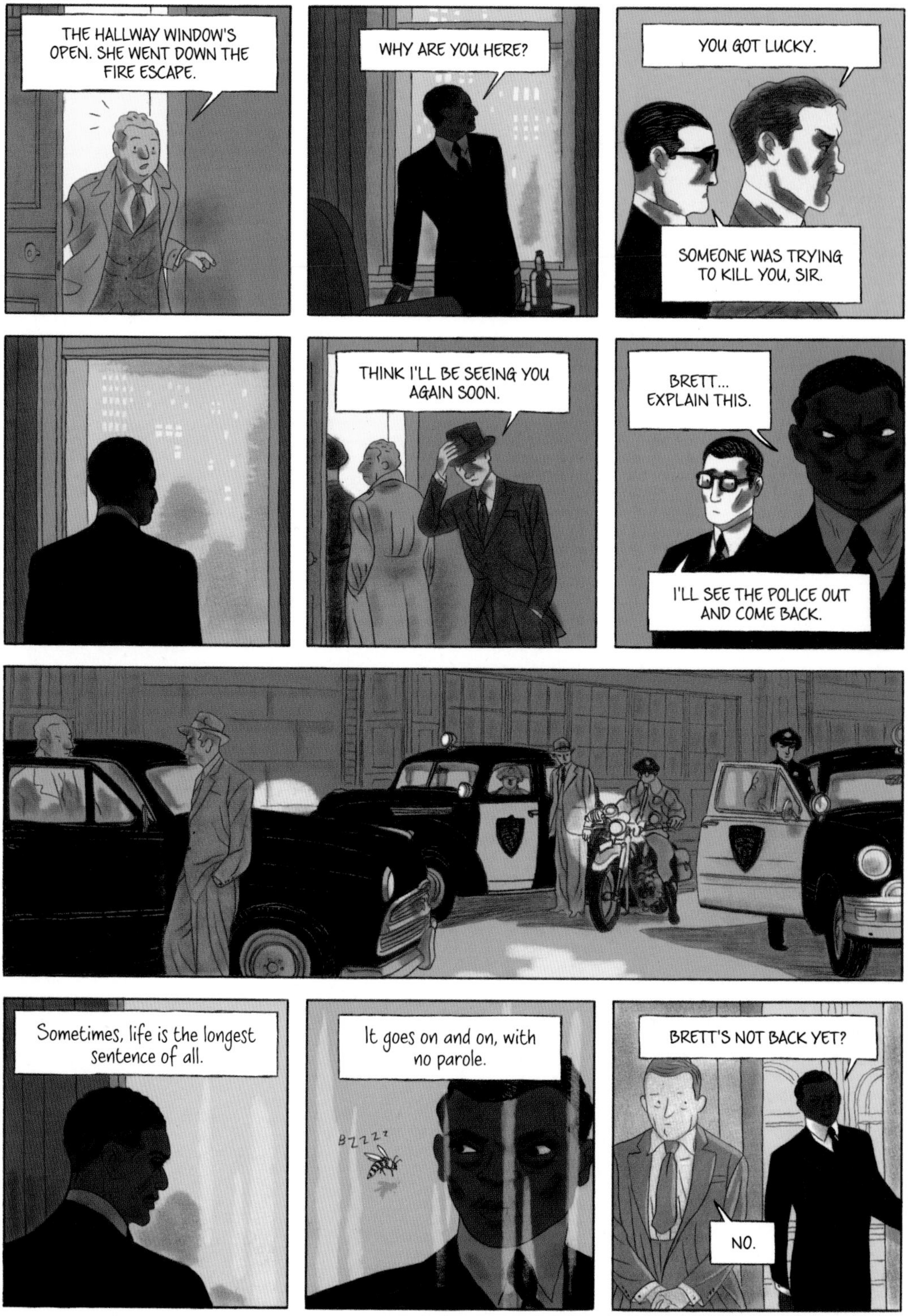
THE HALLWAY WINDOW'S OPEN. SHE WENT DOWN THE FIRE ESCAPE.
WHY ARE YOU HERE?
YOU GOT LUCKY.
SOMEONE WAS TRYING TO KILL YOU, SIR.
THINK I'LL BE SEEING YOU AGAIN SOON.
BRETT... EXPLAIN THIS.
I'LL SEE THE POLICE OUT AND COME BACK.
Sometimes, life is the longest sentence of all.
It goes on and on, with no parole.
BZZZZ
BRETT'S NOT BACK YET?
NO.

BRETT!

BRETT!

I WAS THE ONE WHO LET HER UP...

SIR...IT'S ALL MY FAULT.

BRETT? WHAT ARE YOU SAYING?

SIR...SIR...

WHAT?

BILLIE.

BILLIE!

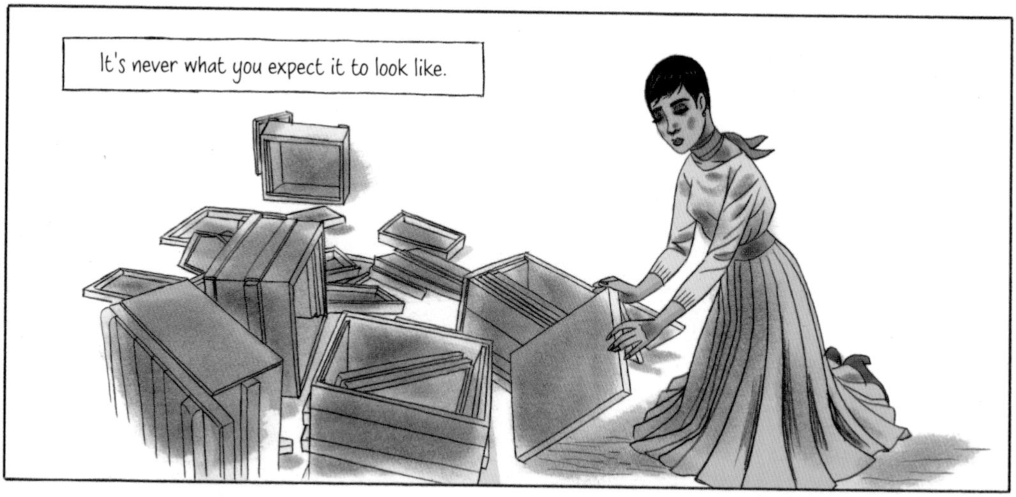
It's never what you expect it to look like.

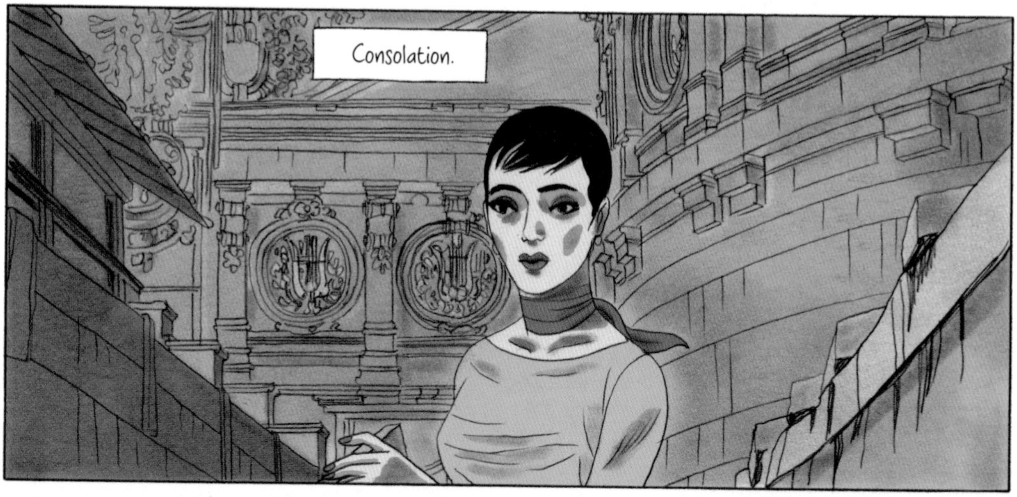
Consolation.

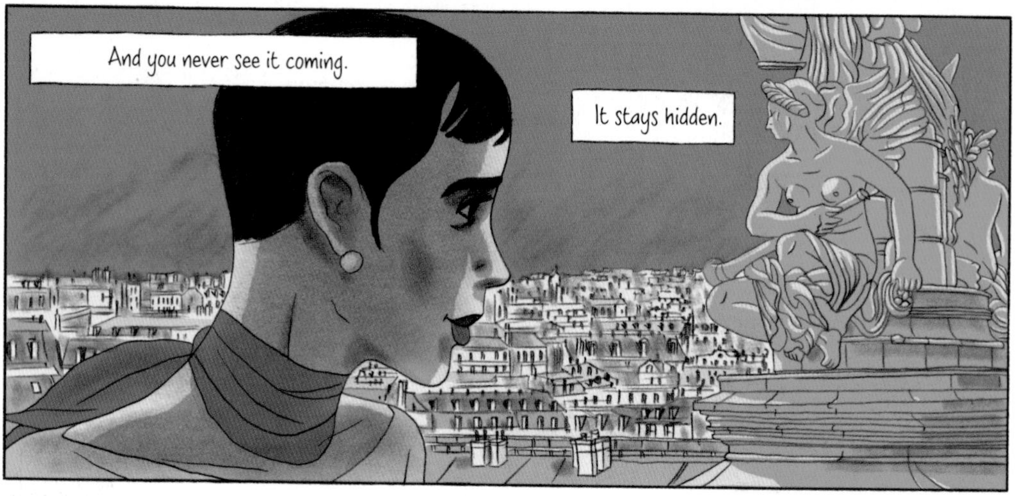
And you never see it coming.
It stays hidden.

For the longest time, I thought he'd left me nothing.

But there was a secret sleeping under the ashes.

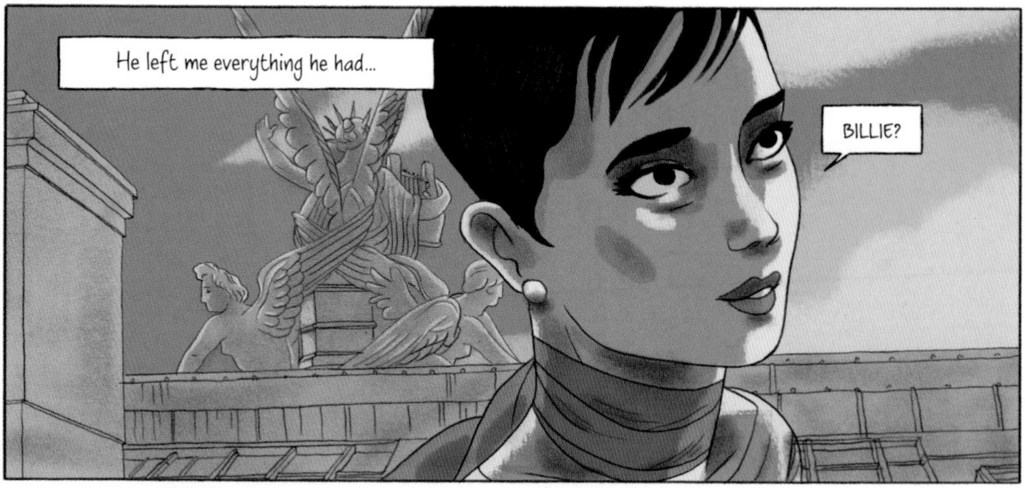
He left me everything he had...
BILLIE?

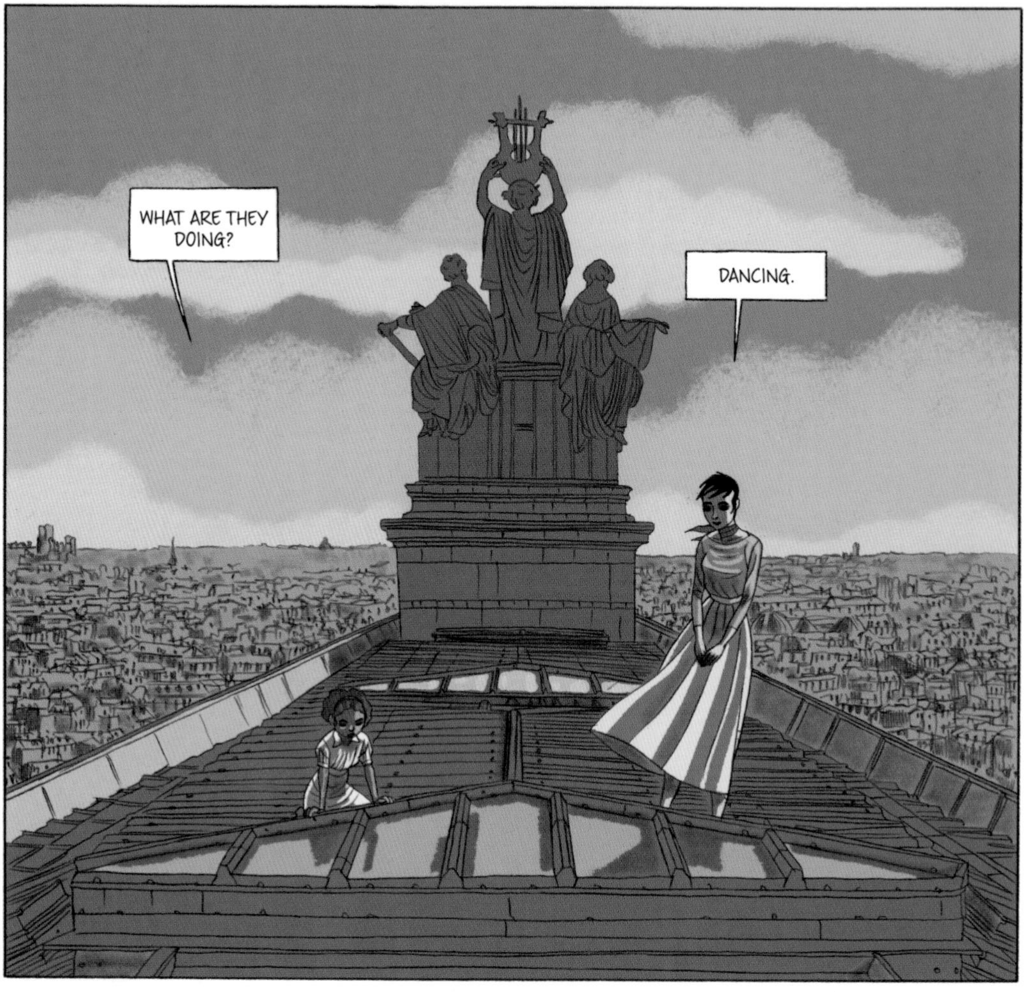
WHAT ARE THEY DOING?
DANCING.